on her first
Birthday

Aunt Gail
Uncle Skip
Andrea, Kat
+ Darren

That's What Counts!

Tapley P. Bear is the creation of Jackie Tapley,
Mountain Bear Manufacturing, Bangor, Maine.

Photography by Margit Studio, Pittsfield, Maine.
Design by Lurelle Cheverie

Copyright © 1983 by Jane D. Weinberger
ISBN 0-89272-173-1
Library of Congress Catalog Card no. 83-70938
Printed in the United States of America

10 9 8 7 6 5 4 3 2 1

DOWN EAST BOOKS/CAMDEN MAINE

That's What Counts!

by Jane D. Weinberger

A Tapley P. Bear Storybook

DOWN EAST BOOKS / CAMDEN, MAINE

This is Tapley P. Bear.

He lives near the woods. He likes to go

camping and fishing

Of course he is not a real, live bear,

but he thinks he is, and

That's What Counts!

apley has three pretty little sister
bears who are gentle, kind, and good.

6

Of course, they are not always good little

bears, but they try to be, and

That's What Counts!

7

oday, Tapley P. Bear is taking some pictures of his three pretty sisters.

Of course, they may not all have pretty faces, but they have kind thoughts and are beautiful on the inside, and

That's What Counts!

There are Honey Bear, Sunny Bear, and Shu-shu.

They are having a tea party, but someone has spilled the honey and they must all do without. Still, they are pleasant and have a good time together, and

That's What Counts!

Honey and Sunny are waiting for their supper, but first Sunny must go to the rose garden and get Shu-shu because Shu-shu has forgotten her eyeglasses. Sometimes Shu-shu is hard to love, but she is their sister, and

That's What Counts!

James is a real, live little boy.
He lives in the house with his mother and
Tapley P. Bear and the three pretty
little sister bears. They all live happily
together, and

That's What Counts!

James is big and strong and brave.
Of course, he is not always very brave,
but he thinks he is, and

That's What Counts!

One day Tapley P. Bear went out with James. They went camping and fishing. After a while, James got tired and went home to his mother but he forgot to take Tapley with him.

There was Tapley P. Bear out in the woods all alone. He did not know how to get home. But he remembered what he should do, and

That's What Counts!

He remembered that if he was lost in the woods or in a great big store he should stay right where he was and wait for someone to find him. He remembered, and

That's What Counts!

After dinner, James went to get his

bears ready for the night.

The three sister bears were having

22

a bedtime snack, just waiting to be

put in their little beds. But Tapley P.

Bear was missing.

James remembered that he had left Tapley out in the woods. He also remembered that it was dark outside. To get to the place where he had left his bear he would have to cross the lawn, go past the rosebushes, past the vegetable garden, and into the woods.

James did not feel very brave, so he called his mother and asked her to get Tapley, but she said, "James, you are a big, brave boy and you know where you left your bear."

James put on his shoes, picked up his flashlight, and went out into the dark. He did not feel brave at all but he knew what he should do, and **That's What Counts!**

He pretended to be as brave as a watchdog and walked as fast as he could across the lawn, past the rosebushes, past the vegetable garden, and into the woods. There he found Tapley P. Bear right where he had left him.

James took Tapley back to his mother
and the three little sister bears.

28

They are happy together again, and

That's What Counts!

29

The End